KU-386-008

Schools Library and Information Services
S00000686921

# Don't Wake Stanley

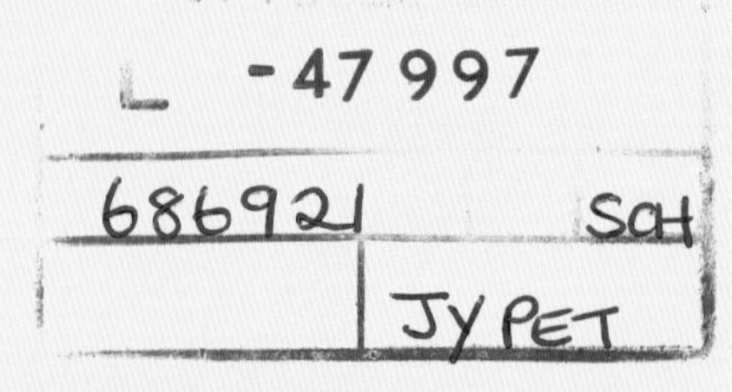




First published in the UK in 2005 by
QED Publishing
A Quarto Group company
226 City Road
London EC1V 2TT
www.qed-publishing.co.uk



A Catalogue record for this book is available from the British Library.

ISBN 1 84538 146 7

Written by Kate Petty
Designed by Melissa Alaverdy
Editor Hannah Ray
Illustrated by Mike Spoor

Series Consultant Anne Faundez
Publisher Steve Evans
Creative Director Louise Morley
Editorial Manager Jean Coppendale

Printed and bound in China

# Don't Wake Stanley

Kate Petty

QED Publishing

The sky is black,
the moon is bright
and all is quiet in
Stanley's house.

Stanley is
fast asleep
in his bed.

Mum and Dad
are gently
snoring.

Little sister Rose is
dreaming of princesses.

In the kitchen, Bert
the dog is curled up
in his basket.

But who is this?

Someone in Stanley's house is wide awake.

Twinkle, the night kitten, stretches, yawns and steps daintily out of her laundry nest in the corner of Stanley's room.

She finds a rolled-up sock to bat about ...

... and wakes up Stanley.

Stanley thinks that if he is awake, then it must be morning.

He jumps out of bed ...

... and goes to say good morning to Mum and Dad.

"Go back to bed, Stanley," says Mum. "It's the middle of the night."

"I'll have to stay with you," says Stanley. "It's too noisy in my room."

“Bother,” says Mum. “There isn’t room for three in the bed.”

And she stomps off downstairs to sleep on the sofa.

Now everyone is asleep again.

Or are they?

Who is this?

It's Rose with an empty glass.

"I can't sleep, Dad," she says.
"I'm thirsty."

So downstairs goes
Dad to the kitchen,
and fills the glass with
water from the tap.

He doesn't notice that
someone else is awake.

"Here's your water, Rose," says Dad, but Rose has fallen fast asleep.

"Bothe r," says Dad.

There isn't room for three in the bed, so off goes Dad to sleep in Stanley's room.

Stanley's bed is
rather small.

But Twinkle is asleep
again, so all is quiet
once more.

Or is it?

What is Bert doing?

Where is Mum going?

That looks like Rose's bed.

Mum is very quiet. She doesn't want to wake anyone up.

Stanley sits up with a fright.
He can hear someone moving around.

What is Rose doing here?

Where is Mum?

Where is Dad?

Stanley goes to look for them.

The sky is blue, the sun is bright and it's time for everyone to wake up.

Mum climbs out of Rose's bed and goes to say good morning to her family.

"Good morning, Dad!"

But Rose is in the bed where Dad usually sleeps.

"Good morning, Stanley!"

But Dad is in the bed where Stanley usually sleeps.

So where is Stanley?

Perhaps Stanley is on the sofa.

No. Bert is on the sofa. (Naughty dog.)

"Good morning, Bert!"

"Did EVERYONE sleep in the wrong bed?" asks Rose.

Stanley?

"Good morning, Stanley!"

Now everyone is awake.

Or are they?

# What do you think?

What time of day is it
when the story starts?

What are the names
of Stanley's pets?

What wakes up Stanley?

Why can't Rose sleep?

Where does Dad sleep after Rose and Stanley have fallen asleep in his bed?

Why is Bert naughty?

Where does Stanley end up sleeping?

Who is still sleeping at the end of the story?

# Parents' and teachers' notes

- Look at the cover of the book together and predict what the story might be about.
- Before reading the story, look carefully through the illustrations and discuss what's happening in each picture.
- Read the story together. Did you guess correctly what the story was going to be about when you looked at the pictures?
- Can your child re-tell the story to you in his or her own words? Don't worry if he or she changes the story, or gets the details wrong – it is the re-telling that is important.
- How many characters are there in the story? (Don't forget to count the pets!)
- Ask your child which is his or her favourite character.
- Can your child draw his or her favourite character?
- How would your child reply to Rose's question on page 18, "Did EVERYONE sleep in the wrong bed?"
- Can your child name some of the noisy goings-on in Stanley's house? For example, Twinkle bats a sock, Dad turns on the kitchen tap, Mum walks downstairs and then up again.
- Ask your child if anything like this has ever happened in his or her family. What noises can your child hear when lying in bed (e.g. the television, traffic going past, people talking, dogs barking, etc.)?
- Together, make up your own version of the story. Set it in your child's house and make him or her the main character. Does your child have a pet? If so, the pet could be responsible for waking up your child at the start of the story. If he or she does not have a pet, what else could wake your child (e.g. a younger sibling or a parent snoring!)? Where will all the members of the household wake up in the morning? Where will the main character wake up?
- Talk to your child about how it feels to be awake in the night.